THE LEGEND OF JACK, JILL, AND THE PIRATE'S TREASURE:

An Action-Adventure Chapter Book for Kids 8-12 with Dyslexia (Large Print)

ADAM FREE

CONTENTS

CHAPTER 1

In the middle of the Pacific—at the center of its rocky courses and windy waves—lay one of the sturdiest and tiniest boats the sea has ever laid her eyes upon.

And what did those who trembled in fear call it? *The Heavenly Rulers' Blackest Pearl.*

...But truthfully, the two who manned the ship with their tiny hands preferred its shorter name: *The Blue Pearl.*

* * *

Jack and Jill weren't ordinary pirates. In fact, to most who looked down upon them, they weren't' considered pirates at all.

Duneport citizens refused to think them old enough to sail, and most of their adventures affirmed that when they barely sailed farther than their island home's coast. When infighting among aspiring seafarers like them, certain crews infiltrated their ship and stole their goods while insulting them. They would push them down and break parts of The *Blue* Pearl—urging the kids to "go home to their Mama" when tears pricked the corner of Jill's eyes. Nasty folk, the lot of them.

Their parents weren't even here in the first place! How were they supposed to go back if the two going out to sea were the reasons the twins became pirates in the first place?! Jack could never come up with a good insult to fling in turn. He feels like he should be thankful he hasn't from the few chances his sister sobbed, though. Something told him that his recklessness could've made any situation worse.

Still, their lives weren't always filled with bullying and senselessness; it really wasn't *all* bad. Some of their outings proved fruitful, and those that did were rewarded with gold coins they could spend on themselves. While Jack was the type to want to spend it right away, Jill often took a majority of the gold pieces and stuck them in a piggy bank under her bed. She wanted to save it for a rainy day, often reminding him just how much ships cost when they were torn to bits after a long tirp.

You never know what could happen to us while at sea, she'd said to him one night. He rolled his eyes. What *would* happen? Trouble barely brewed, and there were times he wanted it to so he could feel like a *real* tried-and-true pirate! t would save their trips from being so boring and restless most of the time, that's for sure.

All the chatter and more leads them to a new day and a new trip. Surprisingly its beginning wasn't boring like all the rest. They went from feeding their parrot Birdy and scrubbing decks to charting a plan to sail farther than ever before. Jack might have been happy to see their wishes were finally coming true, but he had to admit: he was a *little* scared of what could come out of it.

Why was he scared? Simple. He, Jill, and Birdy would find themselves sailing into the murkier parts of the Pacific known as "the Strays" after finding a map in old Grandmother Rose's island hut. Jill immediately got to work figuring out where to go when she realized finding out about it wasn't a dream. And thinking the map would lead them a smidge out of Duneport's view, Jack couldn't quell the fear that welled up in his throat when he learned the trip was *just* the opposite.

"Come on, Jack, the boat isn't gonna sail itself if you stand at the wheel all day!"

His sister dangles off the mizzenmast's bucket-like structure as she shouts to him. How has the blood not rushed to her head, yet?

"Can you blame me for being so scared? We *are* traveling to the Strays everyone's talking about," he whines. Sweat beads his forehead as he speaks. "We made a vow not to go there until we were super-duper good at this whole pirate thing! Dad's written *letters* to us about how he nearly lost *Bond* because of the random sea tornadoes!"

Jill blinks. She flips right-side up and sits atop one of the sturdy ropes. "They're called *typhoons*, Jack."

"Typhoon, Schmyphoon, it's *still* risky."

"Look, I'm just as scared as you are, but I *know* we'll be fine." Her capability to wave off danger never ceased to amaze him. "'Sides, aren't *you* supposed to be the brave one? You've craved for an adventure that involved treasure—and here we are!"

He can't help but sigh; he knows just how right she is, never wanting to admit it to her face. Not only was Jack the one who discovered a bottled map and compass from Rose's chambers, he was also the one who traveled through each of the trails she marked without any worry or thought behind it. The one that had scared off many a vagrant from trying to steal their boat!

He was so sure the items left behind were nothing but a hoax—a *prank* by elder pirates... But even so, there was just a lot lining up between them that made it too real to be. He yields, taking a deep breath before gripping the boat's steering wheel extra tight.

"Fine, we'll start sailing towards the Strays, but I am *turning* around if something bad hits us." Jack frowns. "I want us to be safe from harm at all times."

"You're so sweet, Jack, but we'll be okay! We always are." She proudly puffs her chest out. "Besides, what's the worst that could happen? We've been in lots of trouble before; what makes this one any different?"

The boy chooses not to retort. *They'd be at this all day if he chose to.* As confident as she is, as careful as he would *be*, there was something in his heart that told him this trip was *not* going to be as smooth as it should be. Something in his gut.

And if there's anything Jack knew about his gut, it was that it was almost *never* wrong. The question was: *when* would the bad happen? When and *where*?

Words: Heavenly, Strays, Jack

CHAPTER 2

When Jack's nerves didn't betray him, he was every bit of a phenomenal captain as he wanted himself to be.

Though he had an awful habit of tearing himself down and calling himself the "stupid twin" of the two, his brain never hesitated to do three times the amount of work it normally did when it had to! He could tell how chaotic the current could become based on the boat's rocking against waves, and could identify which hard-to-spot Sea Beasts came close. There was no magic to it, only knowledge. It was knowledge said to have come from Grandmother Rose herself, and he did everything he could to prove just how strong he was to other people. His skill worked in his favor more often than not because of it.

What's more, is twhen Jack had to dock? When he had to speed through brewing storms and treacherous waters? He knew exactly which paths he had to take to get him and his sister out of the rainiest pickles possible. He made sure it wouldn't come to that this time around, though.

Prior to their departure, the Skywatchers explained the weather forecast for the week; no rain for the first five days of the trip, light storms for the remaining three. That being said, the reports never cleared away his skepticism. He told Jill they'd dock somewhere safe if the weather took a turn for the worse—said he'd do everything in his power to keep her safe and well. And with his rudder a flutter, Jack kept his eyes forward as Duneport's dock was once again out of sight and out of mind.

Meanwhile, Jill —known for marking different bumps and creases on the crinkled map at breakneck speeds — gabbed to herself while she treated the map like a coloring page.

She was the humble gal who deserved to act cocky—the brainiac, the witty, the strategic! Not only did was she diligent with taking stock before and after every trip, Jill carried the capability of talking to passing seafarers that refused to let them go without a spot of negotiation. She was a master of pulling the two out of conflict, preferring to establish alliances after trading some goods with the curious. It came to a point where locals of the smaller islands nearby could recognize The *Blue Pearl* before she even had to callout to them. It made negotiating so much easier the more often it happened.

Where her brother yearned to be a recognized Captain, Jill wanted to be a Cartographer. A researcher of maps who could tell tales *and* light a path to new worlds in her own way! "Gramma Rose's" special map was one of many trials she needed to face, taking every moment seriously in hopes of something good coming out of this adventure for the two of them. Maybe even for Birdy too; make it three, and all.

Despite all the formalities, who would tell her brother cute little bedtime stories to help him sleep at night when the boat drifted on its own? It might not have been in her job description, but it kept his worrywart fears away when they struck his heart bad. They kept him awake, they kept him updated.

The tales also inspired him to continue pushing forward. Although not fantastically mythical by any means, Jill's words were more than enough to keep him in his pirate captain seat regardless of what happened between them.

She stops her mumbling after a while, digging into her pocket to pull out Rose's compass; the trinket had four small and colorful gems in a circle across the top, while the centerpiece had a large grey one. She had a feeling Rose wanted her to take it from the start seeing as she left it close to the treasure chest the map was located at in the first place.

She giggles and kicks her legs as she fwips her gaze between the paper and metal. Jack eventually broke her train of thoughts with a comment she wasn't expecting to hear in the moment.

"I still don't understand why you're so focused on that stupid thing. It's *just* a *compass*! I have one, you have one... why is this one any different?"

This wasn't the first time Jill heard him say something so heartbreaking, and it certainly wasn't the last. The rage boils within as she — once again — *tries* to get him to understand that there was more to it than met the eye.

"I've said it once and I'll say it again: Gramma wouldn't leave a compass with jewels that match a map unless she had a reason for it!"

"Okay, but there are so many compasses with fancy gems in the world. Maybe it's one of her silly little antiques she liked so much." He rolls his eyes, turning his focus away from their discussion and back at sea. The girl is sprawled against the floor and fiddles in an attempt to ignore what her brother just said. She loved him and all, but she hated when he looked down on her opinions.

"I highly doubt that! It was in her favorite treasure chest, and that box held *so many* secrets, remember?! Secrets that led to storytime before bed. How could you insult it when it's saved her life so many times?"

She dangles it in Jack's face she would dangle a toy in front of a cat. The boy frantically swats at it, and she immediately clutches it as tight as she can to her chest.

"Jill. Compasses are *supposed* to save lives."

"...You really aren't that curious? You're not considering the options she could've left?"

Birdy chimes in after munching on a saltine cracker. "*Squaaaaawk,* consider! *Squaaaaawk,* consider!"

Jack fires a glare at the bird, who stops after he offers another from his pocket. That bird was the type to annoy to heck out of him when he dismissed Jill's words. He says nothing. She keeps talking.

"Dude, think about it! That story about the ghost saving her from a life-ending shipwreck wasn't fake, you know! She thought this thing to be her baby. A *genius* baby, at that!" Jill chooses to stick her face back into the map; her brother was quieter than the water waves at this point. "She said the gems on it lit up... and honestly, the reds and blues match the dots of the same color on the paper, so maybe...! M-maybe...!"

"Uuuugh! I get it, I get it! The compass is important, or whatever—just throw me the map, will you?!"

To say he was annoyed was an understatement. She tosses the paper at him and his eyes immediately bounce from corner to corner. *They're not too far from the X, he thinks.* He isn't quite sure *why* she's focusing so much on that pesky thing. *Surely* his intuition can get them through the thick of the adventure faster, right? No need to believe fiction and fairytales from their grandmother—no matter how sweet she could be.

He turns the wheel and sail, sail, sails! ...But even when he feels they are safe and sound, there is a rumble in his gut he just can't seem to shake away...

Words: Map, Mythical, Jill

CHAPTER 3

Ugh. Ugh, ugh, *ugh!*

Call him petty, but Jack hated when Jill was right more than once in any given situation. He hates it even more now that the two of them have somehow gotten themselves stuck in the center of the Strays.

He didn't want to believe in the compass— really, he *didn't.* As much as he loved Grandmother Rose to death, how was a simple hunk of junk going to save her life when her life was at stake? None of that made a a lick of sense to him! Non-magical metal doohickeys couldn't *save lives*, it was the power of brains and brawn that would get someone out of a pinch like this... and yet... and *yet...!*

Thinking back to Duneport discussions, Jack knew many a pirate had who told him navigating the area was a lost cause. He recalls them insisting on turning back as quickly as they could once the weather got bad. And even though Jack knew they were right deep down, his pride said otherwise! His gut kept telling him to push forward to their destination! The veterans said it would be too dangerous—they said the rain would "get them good" ...and now here they were, practically knocking on Davy Jones' Locker.

Day three gone, Jill had noticed clouds forming overhead on day four. They practically covered the entire sky on *NOT-day five.* They squabbled and scrambled, going so far as to ask *Birdy* to reconfirm what the Skywatchers said... and boy were they all WRONG! While the professionals *did* say it would happen in *five* days, in the wind was quick to pull and push Jack in directions he didn't want to go in. Turning the wheel grew immensely difficult, and the consistent ripping and tearing of their sails made them want to puke... Jack's heart pounded against his ribcage the darker and darker the skies became. His palms sweat against the wood he gripped against. *He wanted to keep pushing forward... He kept* telling *himself he could push forward...*

It was when the thunder and lightning came crashing down that Jill began to yell at him to turn away; she told him to veer as far to the right as he possibly could! When asking why, his eyes grew wide at the compass—the *map*! The blue gemstone at the very top of the item beamed brightly, and the map flew out of her hands to do the same! He wanted to tell her no *so* badly—to stop her from making jokes...

...But in the end, he was glad he didn't. He was glad his stubbornness cooled it for once. Had he not turned in the direction they needed to go, he would have found them sleeping with the fishes. Literally!

A shiver of sharks was passing through the Strays as the thunder and lightning progressively grew very, *very* frightening; they better not be stuck in this mess. The thought of him being eaten alive made him quake in his boots... his hands couldn't keep their grip on the wheel for a bit, resulting in Jill coming to help him steer not long after.

The storm continues, but calms after a few hours pass. To say the two were soaked was an understatement.

And while he was happy they made it out alive, that relief *quickly* left him when he heard Jill giggle like a hyena did. She skipped towards where he lingered, poking his cheek once, twice—*three* times! The longer she poked, the harder it was for him to calm down, though. He couldn't help but groan and smack her hand away. Each word out of his mouth is an angry hiss.

"Shut up. Stop poking my cheeks!"

She smirks. It's a rather smug one, to say the least. "I just think we should listen to what the spooky paper here has to tell us."

"Yeah, yeah, yeah..." The now blue map floats towards him. He plucks it out of the air and shoves his face against it. Was there *nothing* he could do to say his sister was delusional?

The map never stops glowing. Guess not.

"...You're really telling me this stupid thing responds to the compass?"

It was her turn to roll her eyes. She folds her arms over her chest and sighs. "I know you think I'm lying, but I promise you I'm *not*. We could even go one step further and say it helped you turn the boat with ease."

Come to think of it, the boat *was* easier to turn when they were in danger... Dang it!

He gave in to his sister's brainy logic. What choice did he have? It was the only thing he could do, and the only real clue they had to the treasure.

"Fine, I'll bite... the fact that everything came together when these things burned bright wasn't a coincidence. Like, I could've sworn sharks were only in the Atlantic and Southern oceans. They taught that in school."

"I remember all the people talking about how crazy things can get in the Strays. I'm just as confused." Jill says, scratching the back of her head. A nervous laugh escapes her. "At least the worst is over, right...? Sh-should be smooth sailing from here on out—"

—the boat shakes and quakes! Sudden booms and smashes are heard from the hull, and pieces of wood go flying in the air. The twins tumble and slam against the railing (and themselves) in seconds; his sister has *gotta* stop talking like that.

Jill shouts for him over and over, and the panic is enough to drive him out of his mind. She's on a single knee now, checking his arms and legs for any major injuries.

"Are you alright?!"

The smell of smoke and ash hits their nostrils. How suffocating. Sitting up, Jack pushes her away and scrambles onto his feet to regain control of The *Blue Pearl* once more. As quick as he can, he wiggles the blasted thing. The boat grows heavier and heavier as time passes by.

"Jill, the paddles, quickly!" HE commands. "I have half a mind that those explosions were *not* sharks! Not at ALL."

Jill whimpers and runs to do as she's told. She's grabbed one of the paddles but has a hard time rowing whenever her eyes catch a brief glimpse of the shadow closing in on them. She's scared. She's *really* scared. In turn, Jack finds the fear welling up inside of him the same way.

The boat is hit again; at this rate, they will have to *swim* their way to safety! But if there's anything that has been made clear from the attack, it's that the sudden rolling cannonballs made it clear who was attacking them.

Aye, it was none other than the Pearl Patrol. The cops who were notorious for causing trouble when people they weren't fond of were sailing around the sea...

Words: Storm, Duneport, Metal

CHAPTER 4

When it came to sailing through the Pacific, there were three islands every pirate should know about in the event of an emergency.

There was Duneport, the sandy, palm tree-filled beach that the twins called home. There was Nightingale, a fragment of land dedicated to porting cargo in and out of the Strays.

And then, there was Mistfault, a town shrouded in fog and ugly rumors. While Travelers were told to never go there, the area was, unfortunately, the only place the twins could park their precious *Black Pearl* before it sank to the very bottom of the sea.

Hoping to get the Pearl Patrol off their tail, the twins cast aside all doubts and worries and haphazardly parked themselves on Mistfault's dock after making their way through the foggy scenery. Admittedly, they weren't sure what was going to happen when the people saw. Were those living here nice? Were they mean? It was practically a mystery to the people of Duneport, and those who *did* know refused to talk about it. It felt like a secret club, except access was denied for pirates like them.

Still, as scary as the area seemed coming in, the people weren't the type to flee. On the contrary, most of them rushed over to the boat and asked if everything was okay; they all seemed to come from different walks of life, too. Birdy, who was both caged and tucked away in Jill's arms, slammed against the metal bars when too many people approached them after they hopped off. She offered him a full set of crackers, hoping it would be more than enough to soothe him.

Unsure of where to walk, the two were quickly greeted by a young woman in a maid dress. She gazed deep into their eyes before bowing, apologizing for the "inconvenience" that was their rocky landing! It *definitely* wasn't her fault! Relief washing over the two, Jack and Jill quickly explain their circumstances to the girl and follow her on the path to the island's tiny city.

Jill sings the praises of her brother as they walk. She had to admit, he had a knack for escaping danger without understanding the situation! How was risking his neck so natural for him? How did he avoid all those extra cannonballs?! Sure they got lucky and dodged a few that could've hit them hardest, but they should have *not* gotten out of there alive. She had the utmost respect for him, and it showed when he found himself flustered with a deep shade of red on his cheeks.

It was a miracle they survived. She could only hope that the maid girl who promised to lead them to help would be another in waiting. They needed all the help they could get right now. Every last scrap of it.

For as happy as Jill was to *not* be with the fishes, the dilemma didn't change the fact that the family was now *stranded* in the Strays. They were rooted against its sands with no easy exit in sight. Who knows how long it could take to repair The *Blue Pearl*, and how hard was it to navigate outside of the fog once they got back to business? Very few pirates hadn't made it out of here in the first place, right? And what about the map?! Why did the map and compass lead them here...?

She hated that this was the one time her brain wasn't working right; she felt like a failure. All caught up in the bad vibes, the young girl hadn't realized how long it was since they arrived at a diner. Nor had she remembered ordering tasty foods to eat.

Jill? Jill! Your meal is here, c'mon!

She shakes her head and finds Jack sitting across from her at a fancy table. He has a fork and knife in hand, fancy glasses filled with what looked to be... orange juice?

When did this happen?

"You okay? I hope some meat in your system will cheer you up!" The girl from before happily chirps as she slides platters upon platters of food across the table. "It's today's meal sponsored by the king of the seas himself: Blackbeard!"

Jill tries not to think too hard about the "what-if"s and "how"s. She thinks food would do her some good. She watches a mindless Jack poke at the circular slabs of meat with his fork.

"Have we... ever had steak before?" Jack asks.

Jill shakes her head again, a small smile forming on her face.

"No. It was way out of our 'pay-grade'... or whatever the adults call it."

The maid gasps. She acts as if that's the oddest thing she's heard in her life!

"Really?! Please enjoy to your heart's content, then! Let us know if you need more, too!" She squeaks. "Our crew is known for hunting, but no one really *likes* to eat at Captain Blackbeard's café... No one except the Stray Kids, at least."

Jill pauses just as she's about to take a bite. Jack does, too, inches away from ripping that piece of meat apart.

"...Stray Kids?" She asks.

"*Blackbeard?*" He peeps.

"Mhm!" She happily nods, though her smile quickly falters. "...Ah, should I have not said something about that?"

You've said everything you were supposed to, Yoonie. Go help with the other tables.

The twins lose their voice upon hearing such a booming command. They freeze in place as the maid does as she's told and departs with one last bow. The chattering from the other tables got louder the quicker she approached. Those had to be the Stray Kids, right? They... couldn't focus on that right now. Not when that sudden booming voice was accompanied by rattling chains and stomping feet.

So, you're the landlubber pirate wannabes who landed on my turf, are ye?

The proclamation made Jill feel like hurling. A man—not much taller than them—saunters over in a cloak and fluffy garb. His wide-brimmed hat has a single feather tucked behind a tiny skull accessory. The sheer size blocks his gaze. They don't need to look him dead in the eye to know he was staring them down, though. The sinister smirk was more than enough to tell them such things.

Blackbeard was known to be just as big of a bully on the seas and had escaped the wrath of enemy pioneers in his youth. Legends said he was to never appear before those he considered childish and easy prey. Legends *thrived* on how many folks disappeared when he appeared.

They were next, weren't they? They weren't going to go home after all this.

Jack is the first to "thaw" from his fears, though it's to be expected with how big of a fan he is of the pirate celebrity. The look on his face was practically *asking* for an autograph, but she made sure to kick his shin to stop him from doing so. They were in *hot water*. They were *invading* this man's territory.

Blackbeard cackles and places both of his hands against their table. Quietly, he leans in and whispers.

"I was told a few scrawny birds made their way onto the island... And to be so young, too..." He cocks an eyebrow, turning towards Jack and then Jill. "Mind telling me what you're doing here?"

Jill would normally *not* tell the truth when she feels sweat running down her back. This would be one of the few times she does, she thinks.

Stammering, she looks away. She twiddles her thumbs all the while. "U-Um... w-we're, uh... We're C-Captain Jack and Jill from the *B-Black Pearl.* W-we're here on the search for a precious artifact left behind by our g-grandma, Captain Rose..."

The mere declaration takes him aback, it seems. He shifts away for a moment and looks to the floor — as if to think long and hard —

before turning to look at them again. His smirk has yet to leave him.

"Did you say Captain Rose?"

The two of them blink at one another, then look to him with a soft nod.

"What an interesting coincidence. You *could* say I do. Though before I share my side of the story, I want you to share yours." His hand slides down to his belt. It rests just above a scimitar's handle. "Lie once, my children, and you might not get the answers you're looking for."

They gulp. They *squeak*. Before Jack can even get a word in, Jill starts dumping everything she knows on the guy. They were *not* going to be dead meat here!

Words: Blackbeard, Artifact, Sands

CHAPTER 5

Captain Blackbeard got to where he was today *specifically* because of his lack of trust in people.

It could take money, muscle, fame—or even all *three* to get on his good graces. It was usually rare to do so even if people had what he wanted and more. And with the legends of Pirate Captain Rose's greatest treasure rising in rumors among the greedy, he wanted to do everything in his power to secure it for himself. He had to prove it existed and take it away from the grimy hands of the dishonest before it was too late.

His grandmother—well, "grandmother", the relationships were odd—was nothing short of precious to him. Her adventures and her teachings were what made him one of the scariest pirates in all the Pacific to this day! Intimidation wasn't his intention; it simply came naturally when everyone tried to raid his home and take his things. She always praised him for how easy he was to switch faces with a single snap. Happy and charismatic one way, angry and life-threatening in the next.

When her time to leave the world had come, she left him a letter discussing her treasure. Her *Passion*. Proudly proclaiming that it could do everything a pirate wanted and more, she told Blackbeard to find it once he was ready to travel on his own. She said it was special. He sets out to sea until all his supplies run out for the sake of it.

It was this dream of finding it that brought him to take over the Strays—to live there in peace.

And though he'd like to say he was making good progress with one of her trusty maps she left behind, he also wouldn't be lying if the sudden appearance of the twins made him *jealous.*

Rose never mentioned a second map. *Rose never mentioned a second map!* Why would there be? And why did two weak children have their grubby paws scrambling all over it?! He so desperately wanted to make them walk the plank and take it for himself! He wanted to take the compass too, recognizing it dangling from Jill's neck from a mile away.

...But even if he *did*, it was clear they meant no harm. They were more scared of him than the people were scared of *them!* Feeling merciful, Blackbeard decided to listen to their plight and how they got to Mistfault in the first place. He hated to admit it, but he was glad he did.

A bit of negotiation and talking quickly made him realize the three of them were related. Captain Rose mentioned that Blackbeard may come across people he could love and trust. Jack and Jill *were* those people. They were the ones he'd waited to cross paths with, and like it or not, he would have to help them if it meant that he, too, could get one step closer to finding her *Passion*.

This is what leads them all into his "mansion" (really, a cottage) after dinner. He quickly explains that his maids aren't actually "maids", but crew disguised as such to get him through the stuffiest towns and the sketchiest rivers. Royal parties were unfortunately events he simply *couldn't* avoid, after all. The three have tea and cookies together, the fresh and flowery aroma calming the air between them all and painting a relaxed expression on Jill's face. She seemed the most worked up out of all of them, honestly. Even their *bird* warmed up to him!

He sticks strictly to visit, but takes off his hat so they could properly look him in his hardened, emerald eyes. They were family, they should know each other's faces. He gets right down to business after a few cups of tea have went down their hatches.

"So let me get this straight: you two found a map from Captain Rose and it led you here?"

Jill nods. She's the better speaker judging by their small talk before.

"That's right, and it led us here! We were in a *biiig* pinch and the Pearl Patrol was on our tail, but... then it just pulled us away from them."

"And yet at the same time you know nothing about Rose's Passion true whereabouts..."

Another nod. She seems sad this time around, however. "That's right. We didn't even know it had a name until now."

He scans her from head to toe. He looks deep into her eyes—as if looking into her *soul*—before turning away.

"Interesting. Under any normal day, I wouldn't believe you and have you walk the plank off my ship! But seeing as you have her compass and a magical map..." He pauses to sigh. "I suppose I could tell you what I know. What we've been doing on our end."

He takes a bite of his cookies before he continues; he dusts the crumbs off when he's finished.

"Like you, we ran into a map. Traded for it in fact. Some of the maids have done their best in trying to track where it all could lead, but its ripped state has only put us in circles! The Pearl Patrol didn't like *any* of our shenanigans, choosing to chase us to Mistfault and watching over it until they were sure we wouldn't go out again." Blackbeard shakes his head and sighs. "Rumors from travelers came, and we tried to head to Nightingale for information, but we could never get a place to start..."

Jack winces. "That's *gotta* be rough."

"It was—and still is! We've nearly drowned more times than we can count. At least ten times." Blackbeard snorts. "And nowadays, the map hasn't helped! Every time I try to sail out on the *Pauldron,* it leads us into a circle until we return home! Makes no dang sense to me."

Jill tilts her head. "That *is* quite weird... That shouldn't happen even with the most baby of sailors!"

"Still, you trying to keep sailing despite all the failures is dedication! That's so cool of you!" Jack adds, chomping on the last of the cookies. "Jill is our map gal, but this is as far as we've gone. It's been rough, but we want to keep going no matter the cost."

"Honestly, we would've gone *farther* if said Patrol didn't hit us where it hurt..." She sighs. "Now that The *Blue Pearl* needs repairs, I'm sure we're going to need every gold we have to fix it. Maybe even more..."

Jill was right about one thing: the ship's condition could've been *so much* better. The Pearl Patrol's attack left holes and scrapes; a lot of the wood would need to be replaced to avoid rotting and warping. The Stray Kids could definitely get it done... but if they were anything like him in trying to find the treasure as fast as possible...

Well, it's alright. Seeing as they looked to be the trustworthy type, Blackbeard didn't mind offering up the one idea that came to his head during this entire meet-and-greet.

In fact, he seemed rather *excited* to do so. "I don't think you need to worry too much about the sailing part."

He could tell the twins were puzzled—namely Jill. She had a look on her face that just *screamed* "are you stupid".

"Considering we're heading for towards the same destination, there ain't no reason ya shouldn't be allowed to use my boat, right?" His usual smirk turns into a grin. "Let's sail together! The power of three can do a lot of things, you see."

Words: Rose, Passion, Trust

CHAPTER 6

Blackbeard's *Pauldron* was not much different than The *Blue Pearl*. At least, when it came to size, they weren't. The boat had a sleeker and shinier frame than The *Blue Pearl*, and the plating had door-like sections cut off on each side for some reason or another. When sailing, it felt a lot heavier and slower. But perhaps that was better in the long run, seeing as it could take more than a couple of cannonballs at a time.

Jack's closer inspection revealed that the rudders were replaced with rockets, and that all the paddles were automated and *beneath* the ship's hull. Their flag had skulls and crossbones on it, a design considered "stylish" and "classic" by Blackbeard and his peers. Jill had to elbow Jack to stop him from snickering in the corner, though. This was their pride and join! Why ruin it by being mean?

Deciding to leave Birdy behind with the maids to keep its nerves calm, the trio chose to set sail together the next morning. The mere "voluntelling" of Jill's skills shocked her, though. Just because they both had matching maps *didn't mean* she could figure out all the secrets as fast as possible! Theories can only take them so far! Who knows what the world had in store for them after everything they've been through? After everything they *could* go through?!

...And yet, her worries weren't enough to stop them. Blackbeard and Jack were simply all too excited to head out to sea. Every attempt to talk them out of it was interrupted by their own discussions. *At least Blackbeard was said to be good at fighting, right...?* While she couldn't say the same about Jack, they should at least find themselves safe from harm if worst came to worst. Jack could even learn a thing or two from him.

Speaking of Jack, she notices the boy is practically *sparkling* next to the teenage captain. His idolizing of those he likes knows no bounds, that's for sure.

When Jack stood next to him, his calloused hands whitened as they gripped against the railing. He was doing everything in his power to refrain from rocking around in excitement; that would only make Blackbeard nervous while he's twisting the boat side to side, right? The captain *did* mention the ride ahead potentially being a bumpy one, and Jack did *not* want to cause trouble. He wasn't particularly going one way or another; he chose to follow Jill's directions to a certain extent before taking a risk and heading somewhere else afterwards. Her complaints sent him into a fit of laughter.

Getting to the destination is just as fun as figuring out what's at it! Jack took that note to heart, much to his sister's chagrin. He absolutely *needed* that confidence in his life.

They talk about "stuff"—whatever that meant. She could never understand boys and their want to whisper amongst one another. She heard them laugh and shout about random sailing things but chose to prioritize her brainpower for other things. For other parts of their journey.

She had a job to do right now. She couldn't afford to get distracted.

Despite Blackbeard's speedy steering, the trip was relatively peaceful. Liberating, even. In fact, Jill believed the ride to be *so* peaceful that she hadn't expected to fly off the edge of the boat and into the sea! She wasn't ready for the sudden flurry of shots and cannon fire in their direction!

When recognizable sirens sent shivers down her spine, Jill's anxiety spiked to the highest point possible.

Blackbeard's shouts were loud and rugged. Jack kept calling her name over and over. And honestly, the fear struck her so hard that she simply wasn't sure what to do in a situation like this except close her eyes...

The last thing she heard was a splash before everything faded to black.

Words: Pauldron, Pearl

CHAPTER 7

Jack was secretly a crybaby, and everyone who knew him knew this. He hated showing such a side because he knew the tears wouldn't solve anything, and yet part of him *wanted* to after that could've gone wrong *did*.

I mean, who *wouldn't* cry after their sister nearly drowned? Who wouldn't cry when a newfound friend couldn't find himself out of a sticky situation? Who—and he really meant, *who*—wouldn't cry when the infamous Pearl Patrol caught them and threw them into one of the coldest cells on some random island?!

The *Pauldron*, despite its sturdy build and weaponry, could simply not outwit the Pearl Patrol's joint-effort dogpiling. Seriously, how were they able to get random sailors on their sides?! They hopped onto the hull and climbed up the sides—they pulled out their swords and got ready to fight! And even though Jack and Jill were able to knock a *few* of them back, nothing could prepare Blackbeard for the sudden rocky obstacle that came his direction. He found himself choosing between shipwreck and capture--chose quickly between high-sea danger or high-*speed* danger. He ended up making the safer decision.

If the Pauldron is safe, that's all that matters to me. Those were his final words before the two of them were cuffed and loaded onto the Pearl Patrol boat. Jill was recovered from the water; to Jack's understanding, she fainted from all the shock.

Still, despite all the bad, the stay inside the jail itself wasn't *too* terrible. They were fed stale bread every few hours and were given ratty blankets to wrap themselves in. What surprised them the most, however, is how confident those sea cops were to stuff more than one person in the same cell.

No, seriously. Why did they stick three young kids with an old man? That was just *foolish* on their behalf. They spoke to him with ease; they quickly learned he was a Pacific-sailing pirate just like them.

"It ain't often the Pearl Patrol catches people! They're not very good at their job, you see." He laughs. "If they caught you, that must mean you really riled them up! What're ya in for?"

Blackbeard was the one who commandeered the conversation. Better him to speak than the other two, honest.

"Well, you see, we're searching for a treasure. A treasure known as Rose's Passion...? We started hunting for it after getting a few maps and a compass..."

The group spoke for long time, but the information was well worth the time.

The old man, formally known as Jenkins, was supposedly captured many years ago after trying to go for the same thing. A friend of rose's judging by the tattered jacket he wore, he mentioned wanting to find it to keep it safe or preserve it in a museum in the Atlantic. Unfortunately for him, the boat he was riding was a little *too* small and slow to escape their clutches. They captured him without even batting an eye...

He gave up on looking for the treasure because of it, but they came to find he knew a lot more than the Pearl Patrol thought he did. (Seriously, they even called him *stupid*...)

Huddling into a corner for "warmth", the four spoke amongst themselves in whispers. Not even the guards could hear them.

"If the treasure is what ya seek, you're in luck: it's on the tail-end of this very island." The old man grins as he watches them all lean in. "*Rose's Passion* was said to have landed here after the Captain herself made a deal with the Pearl Patrol. They've kept it under wraps ever since!"

The trio's eyes widened, and their jaws dropped in unison. HERE? The treasure was located HERE?!

"The Pearl Patrol doesn't want anyone coming to this island. To *Elysium*. They act like predators chasing prey because they know just how magical it is, though even I couldn't tell you what the *Passion* can do..."

Jack tilts his head. "What does it even look like to begin with?"

"Some say it's a necklace. Some say it's a ring. Your guess is as good as mine."

"Can we even get out of here?" Jill remarks. "The guards seem as attentive as any, and it's not like we can dig through the stone..."

Jenkins snickers. "Ah, my girl, the way out is closer — not to mention, easier! — than you might think! Though *I* personally can't get out of this place, I know you three can if I give you the help you desire."

Blackbeard cocks an eyebrow. "What do you mean *you* can't get out of this place?"

"Simple!" Jenkins turns and points at the wall. "See that rose and thorn vine scraped against the wall? I think that's the answer you might be seeking. Try taking out your map and seeing if it'll do ya some good!"

Lily blinks, takes one long look at the guards again, then looks back. "But... b-but what if we don't make it out?"

"Oh, trust me." He nods. "If there's anyone who *can* get out of here safe and sound? It'll be you three. I promise."

Though still hesitant to believe every word that came out of the old man's mouth, Jill had to admit she was...quite convinced by the confidence he had in her. It made her wonder if he was always like this, or if this really *was* an opportunity to get out while they still could...

She approaches the wall after a hesitant pause. What she expects to come next after she places her hand against is unlike anything she's experienced before...

Words: Jenkins, Treasure

CHAPTER 8

The Pearl Patrol's prison was as fortified as it could get. The steel was hard to break, the keys were out of reach, and the guards were fully attentive during every stroll across the hallway. For a man like Jenkins, escaping was a no-go. How could he? He was wrinkly, he was thin, and breaking through the air vents just wasn't feasible for him. He had a better chance fighting his way out than falling on his butt and breaking something.

But for the twins? For Blackbeard? Their escape was imminent. All it took was for Rose's map and compass to shine as brightly as Jenkins remembered it did, preparing a teleportation out and away from the prison to...somewhere or another.

Ahn while they were happy to find a seemingly easy way out, Blackbeard didn't feel comfortable leaving. Not yet! All this information given by some humble man, and they were just going to leave him behind? He jerked back to extend a hand in the man's direction, but all the guy did was refuse it and take a few steps back. The guards were panicking and yelling all the while.

" Don't worry about me! I'll find a way out!" He proclaims. Blackbeard wasn't sure *how* he'd manage to get by, but was there *really* time to worry? Their bodies were all but out of the building!

There's a flicker—a shimmer. At the snap of the fingers, at the drop of a hat, the twins found themselves blinded by yellow-white light and brought into a forest they wouldn't have expected to exist in the area. One by one, they all toppled against one another. They fell no differently than a stack of dominoes after a rigorous game. They fell quickly, though without any grace.

And after all the "ouch"s and "yikes" were cast aside, Jill is the first to stand with the compass over her neck like a necklace and the map... *pieced together?!*

Wait. Hang on. How did *THAT* happen? Each of its four corners shined alongside the compass's extra gemstones, and the notes that were so carefully written across the parchment had all but dripped away... It felt cryptic, in a way. Scary. Though Jack had half a mind to assume all of their hard work was gone without a trace, Jill believed otherwise when she saw the many dots and lines from the edges come together and create...a trail.

No, not just that—a *whole new map in its entirety!* She couldn't believe her eyes! She'd heard of fancy technology hailing from certain towns before, but to see a map turn into what was essentially a digital screen was way more than she could have ever expected! It got those happy little brain juices flowing; it sent her in a mad dash towards the direction it so carefully marked on the land.

The boys, surprised by her sudden speed, did all they could to rush after her and see what all the fuss was about. They tried to call out to her, but she just didn't listen. She *couldn't* listen!

How could she, when they were so, so, *soooo* close to what they were looking for all this time?!

Pushing through trees and stomping through swampy puddles, the three eventually found themselves making headway towards the door. Were it not surrounded by a number of different locks, they would've lost track of Jill and likely not have found her.

She's fallen to her knees to catch her breath. Blackbeard quickly takes the map from her and glances at it.

"W-what the—?! What happened to this thing? It's practically freaking out in my hands."

"That's... th-that's what I was following this entire time...!" She pants out. She's exasperated. "That Jenkins guy...? I think he was onto something... I-I think he knew were the ones who would keep that treasure safe or something!"

"And now we're at a door with the map vibrating and glowing more and more by the passing second..."

"Well, what are we waiting for?" Jack asked. "If the map is wigging out, and the *compass* is wigging out, doesn't that mean we're at the right spot? Doesn't that mean we have to figure out how to open it?"

Blackbeard ruffles Jack's hair and barks out a laugh. "Sure, genius, but the question is: how? It's not like we can stick them in those keyholes. It's not like we can just kick the door down."

"A-and even if we could, there's no telling what kinds of traps could lie beyond this door." Jill pulls the compass away from her neck and fumbles with it between her fingers. "No, there's gotta be *something*... I just... I need a minute to think..."

Words: Necklace, Parchment, Shine

CHAPTER 9

The island of Elysium was unlike all the others; not only was the air shrouded by rain clouds, but the ground beneath them was also no different than the glass a child could walk on at a museum or an archive. Whenever they took steps, it was almost as if they walked on the very water itself. When they approached the door, its surface was just as unmoving as a stone tablet or rock formation. No amount of pushing or shoving would get them inside. The locks against it didn't seem to belong to any key they've seen, either.

How the heck were the Pearl Patrol so good at hiding this place? Or maybe, it wasn't *them* who held the secret, but the very treasure they were looking for. It was hard to say... Hard to think about, really. Neither of them believed they were going to get this far, and neither of them had the solution to the problem before them.

...Still, if they were able to get this far, then that meant they had the last step they needed to get what they wanted. It meant that the answer they sought was in the map and the mementos they held in their hands...

Blackbeard looks over the map, but nothing comes to mind. He hands it to Jack.

Jack, unsure of what to make of the gesture, briefly glosses over the piece of paper until a frown formed on his face. Puzzles were *not* his strong suit; he might have had brains, but these types of teasers made his head hurt for days. He passes it to Jill within minutes.

Jill is just as frantic as the rest of them; what was she supposed to do with this? It might be glowing, but what else could it do? What were the secrets that lied within? Was the key related to their memories? Their journey altogether? What could help them? What could get them the treasure they have frantically searched for?!

What they fail to notice in their panic is that each lock against the door has a line against it. A line that could only be made by a hammer and chisel; a line that could fit a word or two if one of them tried hard enough...

Jill gets to work without another word.

Aware that a feather quill isn't the *best* material for what's in front of her, she still tries her best to mark the material once, then twice, and eventually forms a word. It fades after a few seconds. She tries to write her full name—Julianne—and it washes away just as quick. As if tiny little light bulbs pop over her head again and again, she turns to the boys with the widest smile on her face. They weren't quite sure how to react other than twiddle their thumbs and stare.

"I feel kind of silly that I didn't think of how to open the door before... it's a lot more obvious than it looks..."

Blackbeard is the first to speak. The suspense was killing him.

"Okay, so spill it, then! You seem so excited running that silly little quill nub over it, but you're not using your words!"

"As much as I'd like to tell Blackbeard off, he's got a point." Jack adds.

"So impatient! I should just *not* give you the answer." She sticks her tongue out; she knew she would anyway. "Answer me this: what do rocks, ink, and water have in common?"

Blackbeard sputters. "*Excuse me?*"

"Humor me a bit! I promise it'll be worth it."

Jack scratches his chin, his eyes squinting while deep in thought. "Hmm... well, I don't know about *ink*, but I know rocks and water are... things."

"Not exactly what I'm looking for, bro, but I get it."

"They're found in the sea?"

"Close!"

The back-and-forth banter makes Blackbeard fold his arms over his chest. His frown says one thing, but the answer he speaks is another entirely.

"Surfaces. They're both types of surfaces! Although, water is often debated otherwise..."

"RIGHT!" Jill claps her hands. "And what does ink do on surfaces it doesn't like?"

The smarts were kicking in. The boys' jaws drop at the realization.

"They both run off!"

"Exactly! This gate here? It wants us to use words. *Special* words. It didn't want to open when I wrote 'Julianne,' but hypothetically, all the correct words stick! We just have to carve them in!"

"Jill, you're a genius! The treasure is all ours!" Jack bounces up and down. Blackbeard, on the other hand, rolls his eyes and keeps a stern face on him.

"That's great and all, but what would the words even be? There's, like, a bajillion of them. There's no way we're going to get them right."

"Sure we are! I wouldn't worry so much. "Jill takes one of Blackbeard's hands into her own and squeezes it tight. "I think with a few tries, we'll get the answer! In fact, I have a feeling the answer is a lot closer to us than we might think..."

"And you're sure about this?" He raises an eyebrow. "You don't think you're wrong?"

"Nonsense! If I am, you can make me walk the plank or something when we get back!"

The boy pauses. He sighs, scratching the back of his head as he snatches the quill out of her hands. "Yeah, yeah, yeah... Whatever. Let's just get this over with."

She pulls out another pair from her pocket and hands one over to her brother; one can't ever go wrong with extras, after all! And after taking a few deep breaths and hyping herself up, the three work together and begin to list as many words as they possibly could. Where one failed, they'd write again. When two failed, they'd write more.

They wrote, and wrote, and wrote... and — after many a minute passing — it wasn't long until a few of them began to glow. Before the answer was finally revealing itself before their very eyes!

CHAPTER 10

As the answer arrives, the locks break off one by one. The door slowly opens, and another wave of light begins to peek out. The children cover their eyes, but Blackbeard looks directly at it. He watches as a set of shovels clatter to the floor and the map float into the new area that has opened up to them. From there, it disintegrates—turns to ash, in a way. The particles swirl and swirl in the air, eventually landing on the dirt and forming the gigantic X the map was so eager to lead them to.

The compass pulses—the gigantic gem in the middle a shining rainbow before it flies away, too. With newfound confidence, the three of them glance at one another and scramble onto their feet! They rush towards the shovels, grip them for dear life, and rush on in through the door.

"It's here! It's here, it's here, it's *here!!*" Jack squeals, pumping the tool into the air as he does a little dance!

"Incredible. I can't believe getting arrested actually got us somewhere." Blackbeard stated, smug sneer apparent and all. It was as if smoke came out of his nose. "There was *no way* any of us could have predicted this. We really are the world's best pirates!"

"Enough talking, let's get to digging!"

They cheer, they laugh, they squeal. Each of them take turns hauling dirt from beneath the glass-like lands and throwing it to the side. The debris sparkles through the air before landing in a pile. Jack is a bit mesmerized by the sight, unaware that he'd nearly fallen into newfound hole because he pushed his body a little *too* forward.

And, after many a shovel shove, the three uncovered a box. A box they all knew *well*. Bearing the same rose and thorny vine as they saw before, the children watch the compass flicker one last time before attaching to the very top. From there, the box opens!

From there, their journey finally comes to an end.

Rose's Passion was no ring or necklace, but a bracelet. The accessory glimmers with jewels of similar colors, although hit didn't take a nerd to figure out that there was just *something* magical that radiated from it. Blackbeard carefully pinches and picks it up; he inspects it closely. A wide, child-like grin graces his face as he twists and turns the thing around. He hands it over to Jill and Jack, who inspect it with just as much excitement as everyone else.

"We did it, you two. This is it!" He proclaims. "I'm happy we were able to find it, but I really *do* wish Captain Rose was smart enough to leave a letter entailing what it can do for the people."

"We don't have to figure out what it does right now! There's no rush!" Jill pats the teenager on the back. "Now that it's in our hands, we should take it to a safe place! Do you think one of the museums will pay us for it?"

"Maybe... It's no gold, but I'm okay with that!" Jack cheers. "It's what everyone's looking for, right? If we can find a curator that would purchase it, we could use that money for that thing we've wanted to do all this time!"

Blackbeard raises an eyebrow. He tilts his head.

"I hope you don't mind me asking, but... Exactly *what* are you planning to use it for?"

Jill look at Jack. Jack looks at Jill. They share a gaze that spoke more than words ever could and with great pride in their chest, they look to Blackbeard with newfound determination.

"A scholarship!" They begin in unison. "We want pirates who are as brave and as strong as us to go to school and learn the ways of the sea! Isn't that cool?!"

The idea takes Blackbeard by surprise. It's clear the selfless action was *not* what he expected... Still, he likes the idea. Praises it, even.

He likes it so much that he offers to help in the best way he can. He promises to look for someone on Mistfault that could help them get the money they need to start their goal and meet their needs.

The trip back home that evening was peaceful. It felt as if Captain Rose herself showed her pride by leading the boat to them and carrying them back as safe and as swiftly as she possibly could...

THE END.

Made in United States
North Haven, CT
21 October 2023